SIMON & SCHUSTER BOOKS FOR YOUNG READERS
An imprint of Simon & Schuster Children's Publishing Division
1230 Avenue of the Americas, New York, New York 10020

SIMON & SCHUSTER BOOKS FOR YOUNG READERS is a trademark of Simon & Schuster, Inc.
For information about special discounts for bulk purchases, please contact
Simon & Schuster Special Sales at 1-866-506-1949 or business@simonandschuster.com.
The Simon & Schuster Speakers Bureau can bring authors to your live event.
For more information or to book an event, contact the Simon & Schuster Speakers Bureau
at 1-866-248-3049 or visit our website at www.simonspeakers.com.
Also available in a Simon & Schuster Books for Young Readers hardcover edition
Book design by Lucy Ruth Cummins
The text for this book is set in Typewrither.
The illustrations for this book are rendered in pencil and watercolor, and assembled digitally.
Manufactured in China 0319 SCP
First Simon & Schuster Books for Young Readers paperback edition June 2019
2 4 6 8 10 9 7 5 3 1
The Library of Congress has cataloged the hardcover edition as follows:
Clanton, Ben, 1988— author.
It came in the mail / Ben Clanton. — First edition.
pages cm
Summary: After Liam writes to his mailbox, asking for more mail, he gets his wish,
but soon he realizes that sending mail is even more fun than receiving it.
ISBN 978-1-4814-0360-3 (hardcover : alk. paper) — ISBN 978-1-5344-5321-0 (pbk)
ISBN 978-1-4814-0361-0 (eBook)
1. Mailboxes—Juvenile fiction. 2. Postal service—Juvenile fiction. [1. Mailboxes—Fiction.
2. Postal service—Fiction.] I. Title.
PZ7.C52923It 2016
[E]—dc23
2014043694

IT CAME IN THE MAIL

Ben Clanton

Simon & Schuster Books for Young Readers

New York   London   Toronto   Sydney   New Delhi

Liam loved to get mail.

Too bad he never got any.

He checked ~~daily~~

~~hourly~~

every few seconds,
but found . . .

. . . diddly-squat.

But then, on a day much like any other,
an idea struck Liam.

If he sent some mail,
then maybe he'd get some in return.

Not sure who to send something to,
Liam sent a letter to his mailbox.

Dear Mailbox,

I would like to get something in the mail. Something BIG! PLEASE!

Love,

Liam

As soon as Liam put the letter in,
the mailbox began to shake.
It made all sorts of strange sounds.

KRINK

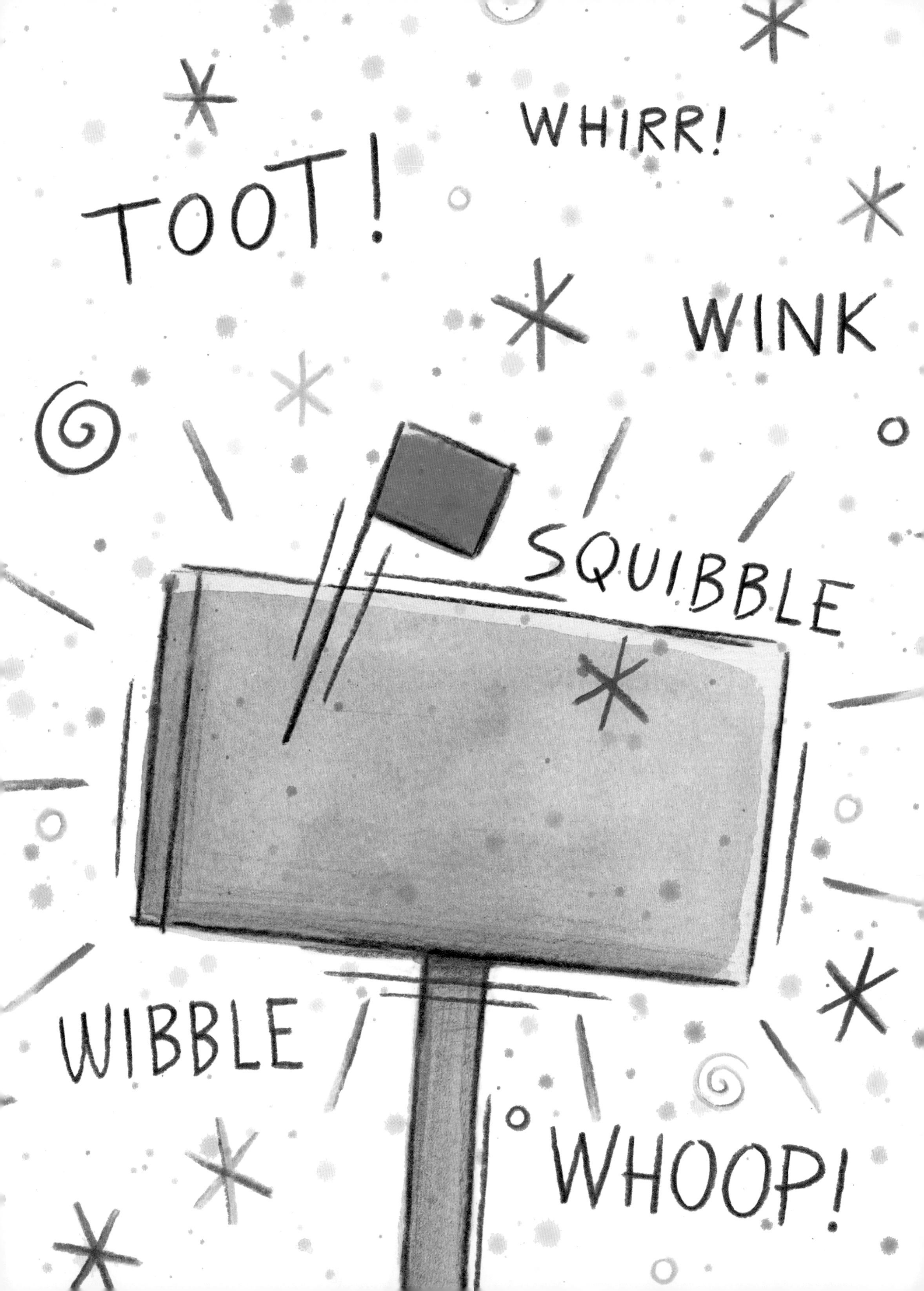
WHIRR!
TOOT!
WINK
SQUIBBLE
WIBBLE
WHOOP!

When Liam looked inside,
he was met by a blast of fire.
A dragon had come in the mail!

And it was for Liam.

Liam loved the dragon.
But he couldn't wait to see what
he might get next!

Dear Mailbox,

Thank you for the fire-breathing dragon. It is just what I always wanted. Can you send me more stuff? PLEASE!
                    Love, Liam

P.S. You are the best mailbox ever!

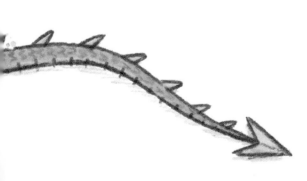

Soon the mailbox was spitting
out all sorts of things.
Pickles! Pigs! A whale with wings!
A trombone! A triceratops bone!
Even a funny bone!

KNOCK!
KNOCK!

squibble
wibble
WHOOP!

Liam liked it all!
He liked it all so much
that he wanted even more.

Dear Mailbox,
You send the best mail.
I would LOVE it if you
sent me a ~~hundred~~
GAZILLION more
things.
Love,
Liam
la la
la

Oodles and oodles of mail
flooded out of the mailbox.

What was Liam to do with it all?!

And then another idea struck Liam.

He probably wasn't the only kid
who had **ever** wanted to get mail.

Dear Mailbox,

Thank you for ALL the mail! ~~the~~ But I think it's maybe too much for just me. Can you help me send some of it to other kids?

Love,
Liam

With some help from the mailbox . . .

. . . Liam was soon mailing things

to kids all over the place!

Liam found he rather liked sending stuff.
He liked it so much that before long,
almost everything was gone.

That was okay with Liam.
He could always ask the
mailbox for more. . . .

But maybe some other time.

FASTER!